Joseph Smith

BOOK 1

CHURCH HISTORY STORIES

LAMB BOOKS

Sight Reading

Joseph Smith

written by Tiffany Thomas
illustrated by Nikki Casassa

CFI • An imprint of Cedar Fort, Inc. • Springville, Utah

HARD WORDS:

Joseph, Palmyra, surgery

PARENT TIP: Choose one or two words for the child to read, with you reading the more difficult words. Each time you read through the story, have them read an additional one or two new words.

This is Joseph Smith.
He is 8 years old.

He has lots of
brothers and sisters.

His mom and dad are good.

They live in Palmyra, New York.

His leg and knee have a big sore.

The doctors cannot help him.

One doctor does a special surgery.

He wants Joseph to drink wine.

Joseph says no. He is brave.

The doctor cuts out the bad sore.

Joseph is all better!

The end.

ISBN 13: 978-1-4621-4470-9

Published by CFI, an imprint of Cedar Fort, Inc. • 2373 W. 700 S., Suite 100, Springville, UT 84663
Distributed by Cedar Fort, Inc., www.cedarfort.com

Library of Congress Control Number: 2024938719

Cover design and interior layout design by Shawnda T. Craig

Printed in China • Printed on acid-free paper
10 9 8 7 6 5 4 3 2 1

HELP your child read while also learning about Church history. Build your child's confidence in reading with the entire LAMB BOOKS series as they progress through each book!

MORE BOOK SETS AVAILABLE IN THE LAMB BOOKS SERIES

BOOK OF MORMON STORIES
NEW TESTAMENT STORIES
OLD TESTAMENT STORIES

FIRST GRADE READING LEVEL
APPEALS TO PRE-K – FIRST GRADE

See cedarfort.com for more uplifting children's books.

ALSO AVAILABLE AS AN EBOOK

CFI
AN IMPRINT OF CEDAR FORT, INC.

CEDAR FORT
Publishing & Media

WWW.CEDARFORT.COM
WWW.AUTHORTIFFANYTHOMAS.COM

LAMB BOOKS
Sight Reading

Joseph Sees God

BOOK 2

CHURCH HISTORY STORIES

LAMB BOOKS

Sight Reading

Joseph Sees God

written by Tiffany Thomas
illustrated by Nikki Casassa

CFI • An imprint of Cedar Fort, Inc. • Springville, Utah

HARD WORDS:

Bible, church, wrong

PARENT TIP: Have the child use a finger, craft stick, twig, or other item to point to each word as they read.

Joseph Smith is 14 years old.

His mom goes to a church.

There are lots of churches.

None of them say the same thing.

Joseph does not know which church is right.

He reads the Bible and
it says to pray.

Joseph goes out and prays in the woods.

God and Jesus
come to Joseph!

They say all the churches are wrong.

"Do not join any of them,"
They say.

Joseph says okay and goes home.

The end.

ISBN 13: 978-1-4621-4470-9

Published by CFI, an imprint of Cedar Fort, Inc. • 2373 W. 700 S., Suite 100, Springville, UT 84663
Distributed by Cedar Fort, Inc., www.cedarfort.com

Library of Congress Control Number: 2024938719

Cover design and interior layout design by Shawnda T. Craig

Printed in China • Printed on acid-free paper
10 9 8 7 6 5 4 3 2 1

HELP your child read while also learning about Church history. Build your child's confidence in reading with the entire LAMB BOOKS series as they progress through each book!

MORE BOOK SETS AVAILABLE IN THE LAMB BOOKS SERIES

BOOK OF MORMON STORIES
NEW TESTAMENT STORIES
OLD TESTAMENT STORIES

FIRST GRADE READING LEVEL
APPEALS TO PRE-K – FIRST GRADE

See cedarfort.com for more uplifting children's books.

ALSO AVAILABLE AS AN EBOOK

CFI
AN IMPRINT OF CEDAR FORT, INC.

CEDAR FORT
Publishing & Media

WWW.CEDARFORT.COM
WWW.AUTHORTIFFANYTHOMAS.COM

LAMB BOOKS
Sight Reading

Joseph and the Plates

OOK
3

CHURCH HISTORY STORIES

LAMB
BOOKS
Sight Reading

Joseph and the Plates

written by Tiffany Thomas
illustrated by Nikki Casassa

CFI • An imprint of Cedar Fort, Inc. • Springville, Utah

HARD WORDS:

Moroni, English, prophet

PARENT TIP: If you or your child begin to feel frustrated about reading, take a break. Or stop and say a prayer.

Joseph Smith is 17 years old.

He prays to God late one night.

He wants to know
what to do to be good.

The angel Moroni comes!

He was the last prophet in America.

He hid the Book of Mormon.

Moroni tells
Joseph where
to go to find it.

Joseph finds it but is not ready yet to keep it.

After 4 years, Moroni says Joseph is ready.

Joseph reads it with God's help.

He copies it into English
for us to read.

The end.

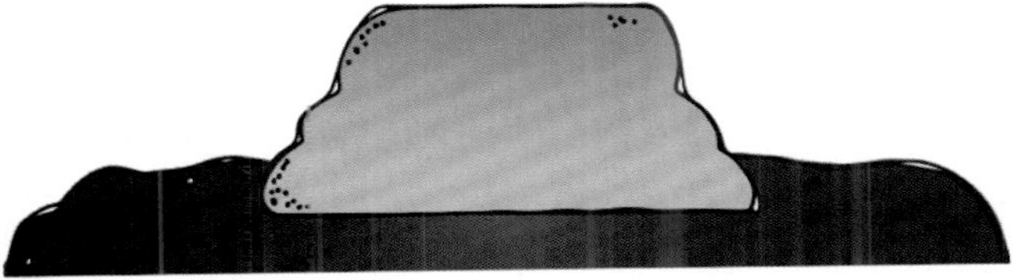

ISBN 13: 978-1-4621-4470-9

Published by CFI, an imprint of Cedar Fort, Inc. • 2373 W. 700 S., Suite 100, Springville, UT 84663
Distributed by Cedar Fort, Inc., www.cedarfort.com

Library of Congress Control Number: 2024938719

Cover design and interior layout design by Shawnda T. Craig

Printed in China • Printed on acid-free paper
10 9 8 7 6 5 4 3 2 1

HELP your child read while also learning about Church history. Build your child's confidence in reading with the entire LAMB BOOKS series as they progress through each book!

MORE BOOK SETS
AVAILABLE IN THE
LAMB BOOKS SERIES

BOOK OF MORMON STORIES
NEW TESTAMENT STORIES
OLD TESTAMENT STORIES

FIRST GRADE READING LEVEL
APPEALS TO PRE-K – FIRST GRADE

See cedarfort.com for more uplifting children's books.

ALSO AVAILABLE AS AN EBOOK

CFI
AN IMPRINT OF CEDAR FORT, INC.

CEDAR FORT
Publishing & Media

WWW.CEDARFORT.COM
WWW.AUTHORTIFFANYTHOMAS.COM

LAMB
BOOKS
Sight Reading

Joseph and Emma

BOOK 4

CHURCH HISTORY STORIES

LAMB BOOKS

Sight Reading

Joseph and Emma

written by Tiffany Thomas
illustrated by Nikki Casassa

CFI • An imprint of Cedar Fort, Inc. • Springville, Utah

HARD WORDS:
believe, marry, family

PARENT TIP: Reading the same books over and over again helps increase fluency and speed.

Joseph Smith is 22 years old.

He goes far away
to work for a man.

The man has a daughter named Emma.

Joseph falls in love with Emma.

He tells her he is a prophet.

Emma believes
Joseph.
Emma loves
Joseph too.

Emma's dad and mom are mad.

Emma and Joseph marry anyway.

They go to live with Joseph's family.

Emma helps Joseph copy the Book of Mormon into English.

Emma is a big help to Joseph in a lot of ways.

The end.

This is not an official publication of The Church of Jesus Christ of Latter-day Saints. The opinions and views expressed herein belong solely to the author and do not necessarily represent the opinions or views of Cedar Fort, Inc. Permission for the use of sources, graphics, and photos is also solely the responsibility of the author.

ISBN 13: 978-1-4621-4470-9

Published by CFI, an imprint of Cedar Fort, Inc. • 2373 W. 700 S., Suite 100, Springville, UT 84663
Distributed by Cedar Fort, Inc., www.cedarfort.com

Library of Congress Control Number: 2024938719

Cover design and interior layout design by Shawnda T. Craig

Printed in China • Printed on acid-free paper
10 9 8 7 6 5 4 3 2 1

HELP your child read while also learning about Church history. Build your child's confidence in reading with the entire LAMB BOOKS series as they progress through each book!

MORE BOOK SETS AVAILABLE IN THE LAMB BOOKS SERIES

BOOK OF MORMON STORIES
NEW TESTAMENT STORIES
OLD TESTAMENT STORIES

FIRST GRADE READING LEVEL
APPEALS TO PRE-K – FIRST GRADE

See cedarfort.com for more uplifting children's books.

ALSO AVAILABLE AS AN EBOOK

CFI
AN IMPRINT OF CEDAR FORT, INC.

CEDAR FORT
Publishing & Media

WWW.CEDARFORT.COM
WWW.AUTHORTIFFANYTHOMAS.COM

LAMB BOOKS
Sight Reading

Martin Loses the Pages

BOOK 5

CHURCH HISTORY STORIES

LAMB BOOKS

Sight Reading

Martin Loses the Pages

written by Tiffany Thomas
illustrated by Nikki Casassa

CFI • An imprint of Cedar Fort, Inc. • Springville, Utah

HARD WORDS:
asking, again, stories

PARENT TIP: Repetition is the key to learning and remembering new sight words. Your child may need to see a new sight word many times before they recognize and remember it.

This is Martin Harris.

He helps Joseph copy the Book of Mormon into English.

They copy 116 pages.

Martin's wife asks
to see the pages.

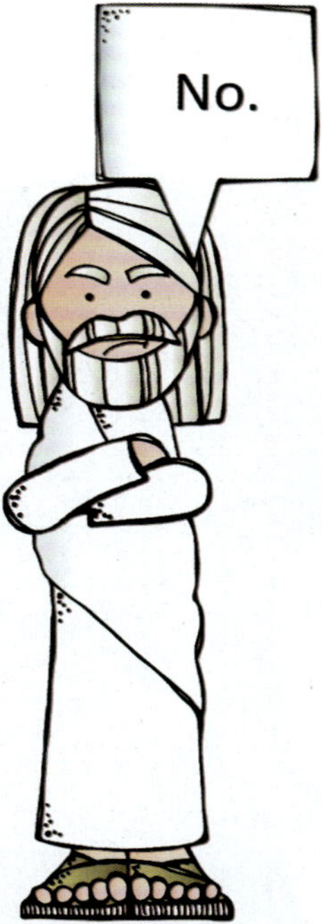

Joseph asks God,
but God says no.

Martin keeps asking Joseph to ask God again.

At last, God
says yes, but
only Martin's
wife can see.

Martin shows his wife
and some friends.

Now the 116
pages are gone!

They are lost!

God says it
is okay.
He knew it
would happen
long ago.

The next part of the book will have the same stories.

The end.

ISBN 13: 978-1-4621-4470-9

Published by CFI, an imprint of Cedar Fort, Inc. • 2373 W. 700 S., Suite 100, Springville, UT 84663
Distributed by Cedar Fort, Inc., www.cedarfort.com

Library of Congress Control Number: 2024938719

Cover design and interior layout design by Shawnda T. Craig

Printed in China • Printed on acid-free paper
10 9 8 7 6 5 4 3 2 1

HELP your child read while also learning about Church history. Build your child's confidence in reading with the entire LAMB BOOKS series as they progress through each book!

MORE BOOK SETS
AVAILABLE IN THE
LAMB BOOKS SERIES

BOOK OF MORMON STORIES
NEW TESTAMENT STORIES
OLD TESTAMENT STORIES

FIRST GRADE READING LEVEL
APPEALS TO PRE-K – FIRST GRADE

See cedarfort.com for more uplifting children's books.

ALSO AVAILABLE AS AN EBOOK

CFI
AN IMPRINT OF CEDAR FORT, INC.

CEDAR FORT
Publishing & Media

WWW.CEDARFORT.COM
WWW.AUTHORTIFFANYTHOMAS.COM

LAMB BOOKS
Sight Reading

Joseph Sees Angels

BOOK 6

CHURCH HISTORY STORIES

LAMB BOOKS

Sight Reading

Joseph Sees Angels

written by Tiffany Thomas
illustrated by Nikki Casassa

CFI • An imprint of Cedar Fort, Inc. • Springville, Utah

HARD WORDS:

Cowdrey, baptism, priesthood

PARENT TIP: Have your child read out loud, even if they can read all of the words by themselves.

This is Oliver Cowdery.

He helps Joseph with
the Book of Mormon.

They read about baptism.

They pray
and ask God
about it.

John the Baptist comes!

He gives them the lesser (Aaronic) priesthood.

They baptize each other.

Then Peter, James, and John come!

They were Apostles
for Jesus Christ.

They give Joseph and Oliver the greater (Melchizedek) priesthood.

They can give the Holy Ghost and so much more.

The end.

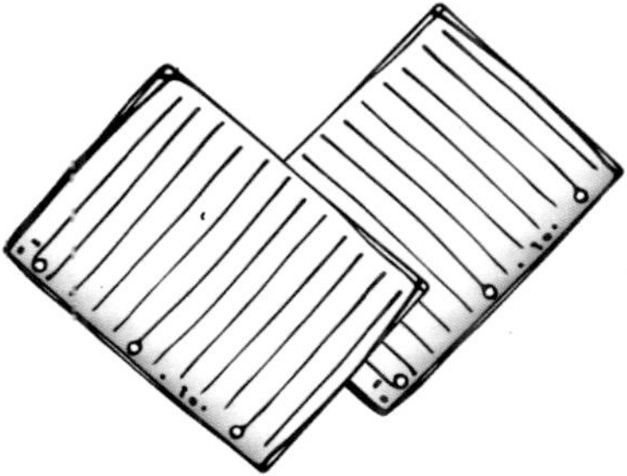

ISBN 13: 978-1-4621-4470-9

Published by CFI, an imprint of Cedar Fort, Inc. • 2373 W. 700 S., Suite 100, Springville, UT 84663
Distributed by Cedar Fort, Inc., www.cedarfort.com

Library of Congress Control Number: 2024938719

Cover design and interior layout design by Shawnda T. Craig

Printed in China • Printed on acid-free paper
10 9 8 7 6 5 4 3 2 1

HELP your child read while also learning about Church history. Build your child's confidence in reading with the entire LAMB BOOKS series as they progress through each book!

MORE BOOK SETS AVAILABLE IN THE LAMB BOOKS SERIES

BOOK OF MORMON STORIES
NEW TESTAMENT STORIES
OLD TESTAMENT STORIES

FIRST GRADE READING LEVEL
APPEALS TO PRE-K – FIRST GRADE

See cedarfort.com for more uplifting children's books.

EBOOK
CFI
AN IMPRINT OF CEDAR FORT, INC.
CEDAR FORT Publishing & Media
WWW.CEDARFORT.COM
WWW.AUTHORTIFFANYTHOMAS.COM
LAMB BOOKS Sight Reading

Joseph Brings Back the Church

BOOK 7

CHURCH HISTORY STORIES

LAMB BOOKS

Sight Reading

Joseph Brings Back the Church

written by Tiffany Thomas
illustrated by Nikki Casassa

CFI • An imprint of Cedar Fort, Inc. • Springville, Utah

HARD WORDS:
sacrament, vision, meeting

PARENT TIP: When your child is stuck on a word, do not say the word for them. Count to five in your head, and then share a strategy to figure it out. (Look at the picture, sound it out, etc.)

Joseph Smith now has the priesthood.

Jesus tells Joseph to bring back His true church.

Joseph has a meeting.

All the baptized people come.

They vote to bring back the true church.

Six people are the first members.

They have the sacrament.

Joseph
gives
people
the gift
of the
Holy
Ghost.

Jesus gives Joseph a vision.

Jesus says Joseph is a prophet.

After the meeting,
lots of people get baptized.

The end.

ISBN 13: 978-1-4621-4470-9

Published by CFI, an imprint of Cedar Fort, Inc. • 2373 W. 700 S., Suite 100, Springville, UT 84663
Distributed by Cedar Fort, Inc., www.cedarfort.com

Library of Congress Control Number: 2024938719

Cover design and interior layout design by Shawnda T. Craig

Printed in China • Printed on acid-free paper
10 9 8 7 6 5 4 3 2 1

HELP your child read while also learning about Church history. Build your child's confidence in reading with the entire LAMB BOOKS series as they progress through each book!

MORE BOOK SETS AVAILABLE IN THE LAMB BOOKS SERIES

BOOK OF MORMON STORIES
NEW TESTAMENT STORIES
OLD TESTAMENT STORIES

FIRST GRADE READING LEVEL
APPEALS TO PRE-K – FIRST GRADE

See cedarfort.com for more uplifting children's books.

ALSO AVAILABLE AS AN EBOOK

CFI
AN IMPRINT OF CEDAR FORT, INC.

CEDAR FORT
Publishing & Media

WWW.CEDARFORT.COM
WWW.AUTHORTIFFANYTHOMAS.COM

LAMB BOOKS
Sight Reading

Emma Makes a Hymn Book

BOOK 8

CHURCH HISTORY STORIES

LAMB BOOKS
Sight Reading

Emma Makes a Hymn Book

written by Tiffany Thomas
illustrated by Nikki Casassa

CFI • An imprint of Cedar Fort, Inc. • Springville, Utah

HARD WORDS:

hymn, lady, scriptures

PARENT TIP: Check for understanding. After a few pages, ask the child what has happened in the story so far.

This is Emma Smith.

She is married to
Joseph Smith, the prophet.

He loves her, and she loves him.

God gives Joseph a vision about Emma.

God says
Emma is a
special lady.

He says
she has
a big job
to do.

God tells Emma to teach the Saints from the scriptures.

He says the
Holy Ghost
will help her.

She is to write, study,
and make a book of songs.

God tells Emma to help Joseph feel happy when he is sad.

Emma does
all God tells
her to do.

She is a
great woman.

The end.

ISBN 13: 978-1-4621-4470-9

Published by CFI, an imprint of Cedar Fort, Inc. • 2373 W. 700 S., Suite 100, Springville, UT 84663
Distributed by Cedar Fort, Inc., www.cedarfort.com

Library of Congress Control Number: 2024938719

Cover design and interior layout design by Shawnda T. Craig

Printed in China • Printed on acid-free paper
10 9 8 7 6 5 4 3 2 1

HELP your child read while also learning about Church history. Build your child's confidence in reading with the entire LAMB BOOKS series as they progress through each book!

MORE BOOK SETS AVAILABLE IN THE LAMB BOOKS SERIES

BOOK OF MORMON STORIES
NEW TESTAMENT STORIES
OLD TESTAMENT STORIES

FIRST GRADE READING LEVEL
APPEALS TO PRE-K – FIRST GRADE

See cedarfort.com for more uplifting children's books.

ALSO AVAILABLE AS AN EBOOK

CFI
AN IMPRINT OF CEDAR FORT, INC

CEDAR FORT Publishing & Media

WWW.CEDARFORT.COM
WWW.AUTHORTIFFANYTHOMAS.COM

LAMB BOOKS
Sight Reading

Men Go on Missions

BOOK 9

CHURCH HISTORY STORIES

LAMB BOOKS

Sight Reading

Men Go on Missions

written by Tiffany Thomas
ilustrated by Nikki Casassa

CFI • An imprint of Cedar Fort, Inc. • Springville, Utah

HARD WORDS:

brother, missionary, listen

PARENT TIP: Find a comfortable place to do your reading, like the couch, the bed, or a soft chair.

This is Samuel.
He is Joseph Smith's brother.

Jesus wants Samuel to go on a mission.

Samuel is
the first
missionary
for the
Church!

He walks 25 miles on the first day.

Many people are mean
and do not want to listen.

He has to sleep under a tree.

He gives a Book of Mormon to Mr. Young.

Mr. Young
has a
brother
named
Brigham.

Samuel goes home.
He thinks he was a bad missionary.

But
Brigham Young
becomes a
prophet later!

Samuel was a great missionary.

The end.

ISBN 13: 978-1-4621-4470-9

Published by CFI, an imprint of Cedar Fort, Inc. • 2373 W. 700 S., Suite 100, Springville, UT 84663
Distributed by Cedar Fort, Inc., www.cedarfort.com

Library of Congress Control Number: 2024938719

Cover design and interior layout design by Shawnda T. Craig

Printed in China • Printed on acid-free paper
10 9 8 7 6 5 4 3 2 1

HELP your child read while also learning about Church history. Build your child's confidence in reading with the entire LAMB BOOKS series as they progress through each book!

MORE BOOK SETS AVAILABLE IN THE LAMB BOOKS SERIES

BOOK OF MORMON STORIES
NEW TESTAMENT STORIES
OLD TESTAMENT STORIES

FIRST GRADE READING LEVEL
APPEALS TO PRE-K – FIRST GRADE

See cedarfort.com for more uplifting children's books.

ALSO AVAILABLE AS AN EBOOK

CFI AN IMPRINT OF CEDAR FORT, INC.

CEDAR FORT Publishing & Media

WWW.CEDARFORT.COM
WWW.AUTHORTIFFANYTHOMAS.COM

LAMB BOOKS Sight Reading

Jesus Will Come Again

BOOK 10

CHURCH HISTORY STORIES

LAMB BOOKS

Sight Reading

Jesus Will Come Again

written by Tiffany Thomas
illustrated by Nikki Casassa

CFI • An imprint of Cedar Fort, Inc. • Springville, Utah

HARD WORDS:
earth, Zion, cloud

PARENT TIP: At the end of the story, have your child act out what was read.

Joseph Smith
has a vision
from Jesus.

Jesus says He will
come to earth again!
We don't know when.

Before He comes,
all people must hear the gospel.

Church members should share the gospel.

There will be signs to
show Jesus will come soon.

Some of the signs seem scary,
like wars and sickness.

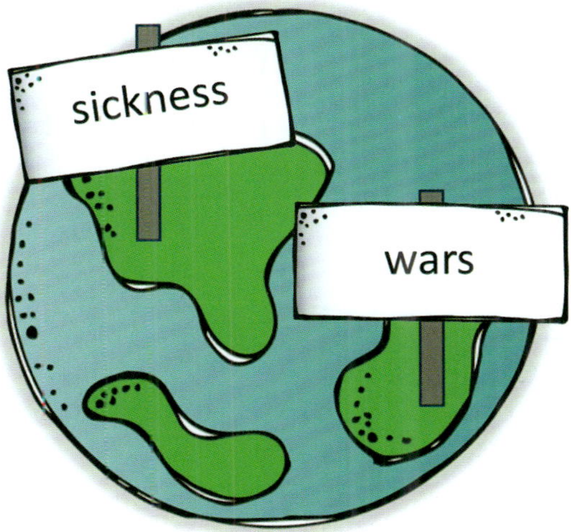

Some of these signs have happened, but not others.

The Saints will form
the city of Zion.

No one will fight in Zion.
People will be safe and happy.

Jesus will come to earth in a cloud.

Good people will be
very happy to see Jesus.

The end.

ISBN 13: 978-1-4621-4470-9

Published by CFI, an imprint of Cedar Fort, Inc. • 2373 W. 700 S., Suite 100, Springville, UT 84663
Distributed by Cedar Fort, Inc., www.cedarfort.com

Library of Congress Control Number: 2024938719

Cover design and interior layout design by Shawnda T. Craig

Printed in China • Printed on acid-free paper
10 9 8 7 6 5 4 3 2 1

HELP your child read while also learning about Church history. Build your child's confidence in reading with the entire LAMB BOOKS series as they progress through each book!

MORE BOOK SETS AVAILABLE IN THE LAMB BOOKS SERIES

BOOK OF MORMON STORIES
NEW TESTAMENT STORIES
OLD TESTAMENT STORIES

FIRST GRADE READING LEVEL
APPEALS TO PRE-K – FIRST GRADE

See cedarfort.com for more uplifting children's books.

ALSO AVAILABLE AS AN EBOOK

CFI
AN IMPRINT OF CEDAR FORT, INC.

CEDAR FORT Publishing & Media

WWW.CEDARFORT.COM
WWW.AUTHORTIFFANYTHOMAS.COM

LAMB BOOKS
Sight Reading

The Plan of Happiness

BOOK 11

CHURCH HISTORY STORIES

LAMB BOOKS

Sight Reading

The Plan of Happiness

written by Tiffany Thomas
illustrated by Nikki Casassa

CFI • An imprint of Cedar Fort, Inc. • Springville, Utah

HARD WORDS:

Celestian, Telestian, Terrestrial

PARENT TIP: Give frequent praise, especially when they keep working on a difficult word.

This is Joseph's friend, Sidney Rigdon.

Joseph and Sidney read about heaven in the Bible.

Joseph wonders if all people go to the same heaven.

Joseph has a vision!
He sees God and Jesus with angels.

All spirits live with God first,
then they get a body on earth.

After we die, we go to the spirit world.

Then God says which kingdom we go to.

The celestial kingdom is like the sun. It's the best.

We go there if we get baptized, obey God, and repent.

The terrestrial kingdom is like the moon. It's for okay people.

The telestial kingdom is like the stars. It's for bad people.

The end.

ISBN 13: 978-1-4621-4470-9

Published by CFI, an imprint of Cedar Fort, Inc. • 2373 W. 700 S., Suite 100, Springville, UT 84663
Distributed by Cedar Fort, Inc., www.cedarfort.com

Library of Congress Control Number: 2024938719

Cover design and interior layout design by Shawnda T. Craig

Printed in China • Printed on acid-free paper
10 9 8 7 6 5 4 3 2 1

HELP your child read while also learning about Church history. Build your child's confidence in reading with the entire LAMB BOOKS series as they progress through each book!

MORE BOOK SETS
AVAILABLE IN THE
LAMB BOOKS SERIES

BOOK OF MORMON STORIES
NEW TESTAMENT STORIES
OLD TESTAMENT STORIES

FIRST GRADE READING LEVEL
APPEALS TO PRE-K – FIRST GRADE

See cedarfort.com for more uplifting children's books.

ALSO AVAILABLE AS AN EBOOK

CFI
AN IMPRINT OF CEDAR FORT, INC.

CEDAR FORT
Publishing & Media

WWW.CEDARFORT.COM
WWW.AUTHORTIFFANYTHOMAS.COM

LAMB BOOKS
Sight Reading

The Word of Wisdom

BOOK 12

CHURCH HISTORY STORIES

LAMB BOOKS

Sight Reading

The Word of Wisdom

written by Tiffany Thomas
illustrated by Nikki Casassa

CFI • An imprint of Cedar Fort, Inc. • Springville, Utah

HARD WORDS:
school, wisdom, alcohol

PARENT TIP: Encourage your child to read aloud to other people, such as siblings and grandparents.

The members of the Church are called Saints.

They want to live near each other.

They all move to Kirtland, Ohio.

Joseph starts a school in Kirtland.

Some of the men smoke pipes.
It is messy and smelly.

Emma does
not feel
good about
the mess.

She asks
Joseph what
God thinks
about it.

Joseph prays.
The Lord says to stop smoking.

He also says to eat good foods and care for our bodies.

He says to not drink tea,
coffee, or alcohol.

This is called the Word of Wisdom.

The end.

ISBN 13: 978-1-4621-4470-9

Published by CFI, an imprint of Cedar Fort, Inc. • 2373 W. 700 S., Suite 100, Springville, UT 84663
Distributed by Cedar Fort, Inc., www.cedarfort.com

Library of Congress Control Number: 2024938719

Cover design and interior layout design by Shawnda T. Craig

Printed in China • Printed on acid-free paper
10 9 8 7 6 5 4 3 2 1

HELP your child read while also learning about Church history. Build your child's confidence in reading with the entire LAMB BOOKS series as they progress through each book!

MORE BOOK SETS AVAILABLE IN THE LAMB BOOKS SERIES

BOOK OF MORMON STORIES
NEW TESTAMENT STORIES
OLD TESTAMENT STORIES

FIRST GRADE READING LEVEL
APPEALS TO PRE-K – FIRST GRADE

See cedarfort.com for more uplifting children's books.

ALSO AVAILABLE AS AN EBOOK

CFI
AN IMPRINT OF CEDAR FORT, INC.

CEDAR FORT Publishing & Media

WWW.CEDARFORT.COM
WWW.AUTHORTIFFANYTHOMAS.COM

LAMB BOOKS Sight Reading

The Kirtland Temple

BOOK 13

LAMB BOOKS

Sight Reading

CHURCH HISTORY STORIES

The Kirtland Temple

written by Tiffany Thomas
illustrated by Nikki Casassa

CFI • An imprint of Cedar Fort, Inc. • Springville, Utah

HARD WORDS:

Kirtland, temple, saints

PARENT TIP: If the child feels overwhelmed, cover the following words so they only see one word. Do not cover the pictures.

Some bad men come
to Kirtland and are mean.

They are called mobs,
and they hurt the Saints.

Some Saints leave and go to Independence, Missouri.

Some Saints stay in Kirtland.

Joseph tells the
Saints in Kirtland
to build a temple.

The men build tall walls.
The women sew.

The kids bring tools and water to the workers.

When the temple is done,
they all go inside.

They sing a song.
Joseph says a special prayer.

Jesus Christ comes
to Joseph in the temple!

He says the temple is His house.

The end.

ISBN 13: 978-1-4621-4470-9

Published by CFI, an imprint of Cedar Fort, Inc. • 2373 W. 700 S., Suite 100, Springville, UT 84663
Distributed by Cedar Fort, Inc., www.cedarfort.com

Library of Congress Control Number: 2024938719

Cover design and interior layout design by Shawnda T. Craig

Printed in China • Printed on acid-free paper
10 9 8 7 6 5 4 3 2 1

HELP your child read while also learning about Church history. Build your child's confidence in reading with the entire LAMB BOOKS series as they progress through each book!

MORE BOOK SETS AVAILABLE IN THE LAMB BOOKS SERIES

BOOK OF MORMON STORIES
NEW TESTAMENT STORIES
OLD TESTAMENT STORIES

FIRST GRADE READING LEVEL
APPEALS TO PRE-K – FIRST GRADE

See cedarfort.com for more uplifting children's books.

ALSO AVAILABLE AS AN EBOOK

CFI
AN IMPRINT OF CEDAR FORT, INC.

CEDAR FORT
Publishing & Media

WWW.CEDARFORT.COM
WWW.AUTHORTIFFANYTHOMAS.COM

LAMB BOOKS
Sight Reading

The Name of the Church

BOOK 14

LAMB BOOKS

Sight Reading

CHURCH HISTORY STORIES

The Name of the Church

written by Tiffany Thomas
illustrated by Nikki Casassa

CFI • An imprint of Cedar Fort, Inc. • Springville, Utah

HARD WORDS:
Latter, saints, worship

PARENT TIP: Have a special celebration the first time a child reads an entire book without help.

Joseph wants to know
what to call the Church.

Lots of people call it
the Mormon Church.

Some don't think the Saints believe in Jesus.

Joseph says
a prayer
to the Lord.

The Lord tells Joseph what the name should be:

The Church of Jesus Christ of Latter-day Saints.

This is Jesus's church, so it needs to have His name.

"Latter-day" means it's right before Christ comes again.

"Saints" means the members try to follow Jesus.

We believe
that
Jesus Christ
is the
Son of God.

We worship Jesus Christ, and we want others to know.

The end.

ISBN 13: 978-1-4621-4470-9

Published by CFI, an imprint of Cedar Fort, Inc. • 2373 W. 700 S., Suite 100, Springville, UT 84663
Distributed by Cedar Fort, Inc., www.cedarfort.com

Library of Congress Control Number: 2024938719

Cover design and interior layout design by Shawnda T. Craig

Printed in China • Printed on acid-free paper
10 9 8 7 6 5 4 3 2 1

HELP your child read while also learning about Church history. Build your child's confidence in reading with the entire LAMB BOOKS series as they progress through each book!

MORE BOOK SETS AVAILABLE IN THE LAMB BOOKS SERIES

BOOK OF MORMON STORIES
NEW TESTAMENT STORIES
OLD TESTAMENT STORIES

FIRST GRADE READING LEVEL
APPEALS TO PRE-K – FIRST GRADE

See cedarfort.com for more uplifting children's books.

ALSO AVAILABLE AS AN EBOOK

CFI
AN IMPRINT OF CEDAR FORT, INC

CEDAR FORT
Publishing & Media

WWW.CEDARFORT.COM
WWW.AUTHORTIFFANYTHOMAS.COM

LAMB BOOKS
Sight Reading

Tithing

BOOK 15

CHURCH HISTORY STORIES

LAMB BOOKS

Sight Reading

Tithing

written by Tiffany Thomas
ilustrated by Nikki Casassa

CFI • An mprint of Cedar Fort, Inc. • Springville, Utah

HARD WORDS:
tithing, chicken, pennies

PARENT TIP: Do not push a child to read so much that they develop reading fatigue.

1¢
1¢
1¢

Joseph reads about tithing in the Bible.

Joseph prays to ask more about tithing.

The Lord tells Joseph the Saints should pay tithing.

He says they should pay God
one tenth of all they have.

If they have ten pennies,
they should pay one penny.

If their chicken lays ten eggs,
they should give one egg.

The Saints pay tithing with money, milk, hay, and other things.

We pay tithing today too. We pay one tenth like the Saints.

Tithing is used to build temples, print scriptures, and help people.

God asks us
to pay a
full tithe.
We give
it to
the bishop.

We get lots of blessings from heaven if we pay tithing.

The end.

ISBN 13: 978-1-4621-4470-9

Published by CFI, an imprint of Cedar Fort, Inc. • 2373 W. 700 S., Suite 100, Springville, UT 84663
Distributed by Cedar Fort, Inc., www.cedarfort.com

Library of Congress Control Number: 2024938719

Cover design and interior layout design by Shawnda T. Craig

Printed in China • Printed on acid-free paper
10 9 8 7 6 5 4 3 2 1

HELP your child read while also learning about Church history. Build your child's confidence in reading with the entire LAMB BOOKS series as they progress through each book!

MORE BOOK SETS AVAILABLE IN THE LAMB BOOKS SERIES

BOOK OF MORMON STORIES
NEW TESTAMENT STORIES
OLD TESTAMENT STORIES

FIRST GRADE READING LEVEL
APPEALS TO PRE-K – FIRST GRADE

See cedarfort.com for more uplifting children's books.

EBOOK

CFI
AN IMPRINT OF CEDAR FORT, INC.

CEDAR FORT Publishing & Media

WWW.CEDARFORT.COM
WWW.AUTHORTIFFANYTHOMAS.COM

LAMB BOOKS
Sight Reading

Mary and Caroline Save the Scriptures

BOOK 16

CHURCH HISTORY STORIES

LAMB BOOKS

Sight Reading

Mary and Caroline Save the Scriptures

written by Tiffany Thomas
illustrated by Nikki Casassa

CFI • An imprint of Cedar Fort, Inc. • Springville, Utah

HARD WORDS:

Independence, Missouri, cornfield

PARENT TIP: If the child struggles with blending consonants, try saying other words with those same blends. Example: brings, bread, brake, brown.

There are lots of missionaries now.

Some of the missionaries go to Missouri.

Lots of people get baptized and go to Independence.

Other people move to Independence to be near the Saints.

Some people are mad
the Saints are coming.

They start another mob
and attack the Saints.

They try to ruin the place where they print the scriptures.

Two girls, Mary and Caroline,
run and get the papers.

They hide in a cornfield and put the papers under them.

The men look but can't find them!

Mary and Caroline save the scriptures!

The end.

ISBN 13: 978-1-4621-4470-9

Published by CFI, an imprint of Cedar Fort, Inc. • 2373 W. 700 S., Suite 100, Springville, UT 84663
Distributed by Cedar Fort, Inc., www.cedarfort.com

Library of Congress Control Number: 2024938719

Cover design and interior layout design by Shawnda T. Craig

Printed in China • Printed on acid-free paper
10 9 8 7 6 5 4 3 2 1

HELP your child read while also learning about Church history. Build your child's confidence in reading with the entire LAMB BOOKS series as they progress through each book!

MORE BOOK SETS AVAILABLE IN THE LAMB BOOKS SERIES

BOOK OF MORMON STORIES
NEW TESTAMENT STORIES
OLD TESTAMENT STORIES

FIRST GRADE READING LEVEL
APPEALS TO PRE-K – FIRST GRADE

See cedarfort.com for more uplifting children's books.

EBOOK

CFI
AN IMPRINT OF CEDAR FORT, INC.

CEDAR FORT
Publishing & Media

WWW.CEDARFORT.COM
WWW.AUTHORTIFFANYTHOMAS.COM

LAMB BOOKS
Sight Reading

Zion's Camp

BOOK 17

CHURCH HISTORY STORIES

LAMB BOOKS

Sight Reading

Zion's Camp

written by Tiffany Thomas
illustrated by Nikki Casassa

CFI • An imprint of Cedar Fort, Inc. • Springville, Utah

HARD WORDS:
miles, water, repent

PARENT TIP: Practice the "silent e" rule in words with and without the e (cut/ cute, mat/ mate, bit/bite, rot/rote).

A mob makes the Saints leave Independence, Missouri.

Joseph is
in Kirtland.
He prays to
ask God
what to do.

God says to take 500 men to Missouri to get their land back.

Only 100 men go.
They are called Zion's Camp.

They walk 35 miles every day and go 1,000 miles!

There isn't much good food or water. Some men get mad.

Joseph tells them to repent
or they will get sick and die.

Lots of men are good and obey.

At last, the camp gets
to a river by Missouri.

A mob is on the other side.
God sends a big storm.

The mob runs away.
No one is hurt!
God saves Zion's Camp.

The end.

ISBN 13: 978-1-4621-4470-9

Published by CFI, an imprint of Cedar Fort, Inc. • 2373 W. 700 S., Suite 100, Springville, UT 84663
Distributed by Cedar Fort, Inc., www.cedarfort.com

Library of Congress Control Number: 2024938719

Cover design and interior layout design by Shawnda T. Craig

Printed in China • Printed on acid-free paper
10 9 8 7 6 5 4 3 2 1

HELP your child read while also learning about Church history. Build your child's confidence in reading with the entire LAMB BOOKS series as they progress through each book!

MORE BOOK SETS AVAILABLE IN THE LAMB BOOKS SERIES

BOOK OF MORMON STORIES
NEW TESTAMENT STORIES
OLD TESTAMENT STORIES

FIRST GRADE READING LEVEL
APPEALS TO PRE-K – FIRST GRADE

See cedarfort.com for more uplifting children's books.

EBOOK

CFI
AN IMPRINT OF CEDAR FORT, INC.

CEDAR FORT
Publishing & Media

WWW.CEDARFORT.COM
WWW.AUTHORTIFFANYTHOMAS.COM

LAMB BOOKS
Sight Reading

Mobs Attack the Saints

BOOK 18

LAMB BOOKS

Sight Reading

CHURCH HISTORY STORIES

Mobs Attack the Saints

written by Tiffany Thomas
illustrated by Nikki Casassa

CFI • An imprint of Cedar Fort, Inc. • Springville, Utah

HARD WORDS:

women, Illinois, Nauvoo

PARENT TIP: Explain that "q" almost always is paired with the letter "u" in a word.

The Saints are in lots of places, like Kirtland and Independence.

Mobs make the
Saints leave Kirtland.

The Saints go to
Far West, Missouri.

Soon the people in Far West make more mobs.

The mobs attack the Saints in Far West.

Many men are beaten and hurt.

The mobs hurt the women and kids too.

Some people are even killed.

The Saints begin to leave Missouri. It is very cold.

They cross the river
into Illinois in the winter.

The Saints start a new city called Nauvoo.

The end.

ISBN 13: 978-1-4621-4470-9

Published by CFI, an imprint of Cedar Fort, Inc. • 2373 W. 700 S., Suite 100, Springville, UT 84663
Distributed by Cedar Fort, Inc., www.cedarfort.com

Library of Congress Control Number: 2024938719

Cover design and interior layout design by Shawnda T. Craig

Printed in China • Printed on acid-free paper
10 9 8 7 6 5 4 3 2 1

HELP your child read while also learning about Church history. Build your child's confidence in reading with the entire LAMB BOOKS series as they progress through each book!

MORE BOOK SETS AVAILABLE IN THE LAMB BOOKS SERIES

BOOK OF MORMON STORIES
NEW TESTAMENT STORIES
OLD TESTAMENT STORIES

FIRST GRADE READING LEVEL
APPEALS TO PRE-K – FIRST GRADE

See cedarfort.com for more uplifting children's books.

EBOOK
CFI
AN IMPRINT OF CEDAR FORT, INC.
CEDAR FORT Publishing & Media
WWW.CEDARFORT.COM
WWW.AUTHORTIFFANYTHOMAS.COM
LAMB BOOKS Sight Reading

Joseph Goes to Jail

BOOK 19

CHURCH HISTORY STORIES

LAMB BOOKS

Sight Reading

Joseph Goes to Jail

written by Tiffany Thomas
illustrated by Nikki Casassa

CFI • An imprint of Cedar Fort, Inc. • Springville, Utah

HARD WORDS:
Liberty, peace, jail

PARENT TIP: There are many double letters in this story: pretty, marry, all. Point out that your child does not have to say the letter two times.

A mob catches Joseph and puts him in jail.

It is called Liberty Jail. Some of his friends are with him.

It is very cold.
There is no fire to stay warm.

They have to
sleep on the floor.

The food is bad and
makes them sick.

Joseph is sad.

He does not
know if he
will go free.

He prays.

Jesus talks
to Joseph.
He says to
have peace.

Jesus tells Joseph to have faith so he will be blessed.

Jesus says not to be scared.
Jesus is stronger than men.

Jesus felt all of our hurts and pains.
They can help us learn.

Joseph
feels better
because
Jesus is
with him.

The end.

ISBN 13: 978-1-4621-4470-9

Published by CFI, an imprint of Cedar Fort, Inc. • 2373 W. 700 S., Suite 100, Springville, UT 84663
Distributed by Cedar Fort, Inc., www.cedarfort.com

Library of Congress Control Number: 2024938719

Cover design and interior layout design by Shawnda T. Craig

Printed in China • Printed on acid-free paper
10 9 8 7 6 5 4 3 2 1

HELP your child read while also learning about Church history. Build your child's confidence in reading with the entire LAMB BOOKS series as they progress through each book!

MORE BOOK SETS
AVAILABLE IN THE
LAMB BOOKS SERIES

BOOK OF MORMON STORIES
NEW TESTAMENT STORIES
OLD TESTAMENT STORIES

FIRST GRADE READING LEVEL
APPEALS TO PRE-K – FIRST GRADE

See cedarfort.com for more uplifting children's books.

CFI
AN IMPRINT OF CEDAR FORT, INC.

CEDAR FORT
Publishing & Media

WWW.CEDARFORT.COM
WWW.AUTHORTIFFANYTHOMAS.COM

LAMB
BOOKS
Sight Reading

The Nauvoo Temple

BOOK 20

CHURCH HISTORY STORIES

LAMB BOOKS

Sight Reading

The Nauvoo Temple

written by Tiffany Thomas
illustrated by Nikki Casassa

CFI • An imprint of Cedar Fort, Inc. • Springville, Utah

HARD WORDS:

swamp, promise, working

PARENT TIP: Point out that two, too, and to are three different words that sound the same, but each different meaning has a different spelling.

Joseph gets out of jail
and looks for the Saints.

He goes to Nauvoo,
which is a swamp.

The Saints are working hard to make Nauvoo nice.

Jesus tells
Joseph they
need to
build a temple.

If they build a
temple, Jesus
will visit it.

In the temple, they can be baptized for the dead.

They can also make more promises with God.

The men and women
all work hard.

The temple is by a big river.

They carve suns and stars
into the stone of the temple.

The temple is almost done!

The end.

ISBN 13: 978-1-4621-4470-9

Published by CFI, an imprint of Cedar Fort, Inc. • 2373 W. 700 S., Suite 100, Springville, UT 84663
Distributed by Cedar Fort, Inc., www.cedarfort.com

Library of Congress Control Number: 2024938719

Cover design and interior layout design by Shawnda T. Craig

Printed in China • Printed on acid-free paper
10 9 8 7 6 5 4 3 2 1

HELP your child read while also learning about Church history. Build your child's confidence in reading with the entire LAMB BOOKS series as they progress through each book!

MORE BOOK SETS AVAILABLE IN THE LAMB BOOKS SERIES

BOOK OF MORMON STORIES
NEW TESTAMENT STORIES
OLD TESTAMENT STORIES

FIRST GRADE READING LEVEL
APPEALS TO PRE-K – FIRST GRADE

See cedarfort.com for more uplifting children's books.

ALSO AVAILABLE AS AN EBOOK

CFI
AN IMPRINT OF CEDAR FORT, INC.

CEDAR FORT Publishing & Media

WWW.CEDARFORT.COM
WWW.AUTHORTIFFANYTHOMAS.COM

LAMB BOOKS
Sight Reading

The Women Help

BOOK 21

CHURCH HISTORY STORIES

LAMB BOOKS

Sight Reading

The Women Help

written by Tiffany Thomas
illustrated by Nikki Casassa

CFI • An imprint of Cedar Fort, Inc. • Springville, Utah

HARD WORDS:
sister, president, society

PARENT TIP: The illustrations on each page will help your child understand and learn the words.

The women want to help. Joseph prays to ask how.

God tells Joseph to start the Relief Society.

This is a group of all the women in the Church.

The Saints who
are women all join.

They help each other,
the sick, and the poor.

The women work hard to help build the temple.

They sew curtains and
make food for the builders.

Emma Smith
is the first
president of
the Relief
Society.

Eliza R. Snow writes the rules for it.

The Relief Society is still here today!

Women are some of God's best helpers.

The end.

ISBN 13: 978-1-4621-4470-9

Published by CFI, an imprint of Cedar Fort, Inc. • 2373 W. 700 S., Suite 100, Springville, UT 84663
Distributed by Cedar Fort, Inc., www.cedarfort.com

Library of Congress Control Number: 2024938719

Cover design and interior layout design by Shawnda T. Craig

Printed in China • Printed on acid-free paper
10 9 8 7 6 5 4 3 2 1

HELP your child read while also learning about Church history. Build your child's confidence in reading with the entire LAMB BOOKS series as they progress through each book!

MORE BOOK SETS AVAILABLE IN THE LAMB BOOKS SERIES

BOOK OF MORMON STORIES
NEW TESTAMENT STORIES
OLD TESTAMENT STORIES

FIRST GRADE READING LEVEL
APPEALS TO PRE-K – FIRST GRADE

See cedarfort.com for more uplifting children's books.

ALSO AVAILABLE AS AN EBOOK

CFI
AN IMPRINT OF CEDAR FORT, INC

CEDAR FORT
Publishing & Media

WWW.CEDARFORT.COM
WWW.AUTHORTIFFANYTHOMAS.COM

LAMB BOOKS
Sight Reading

Eternal Families

BOOK 22

CHURCH HISTORY STORIES

LAMB BOOKS

Sight Reading

Eternal Families

written by Tiffany Thomas
illustrated by Nikki Casassa

CFI • An imprint of Cedar Fort, Inc. • Springville, Utah

HARD WORDS:
eternal, family, someone

PARENT TIP: Point out spaces between words and all of the different punctuation marks.

Joseph asks
the Lord
about marriage.

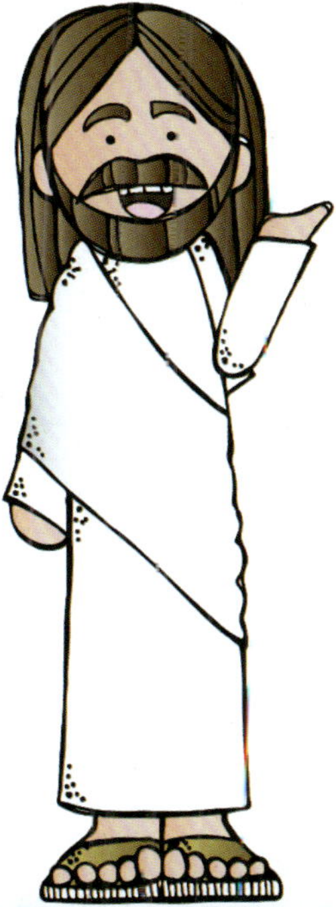

Jesus says
families can
be eternal.

A man and woman can get married in the temple

by someone with
the priesthood.

If they obey God, they will be married forever.

Their kids will be part of their family forever too.

They will be an eternal family in the celestial kingdom.

Joseph sees his brother Alvin there. But Alvin died before being baptized.

Many of Joseph and Emma's babies had died too.

The Lord says all people with good hearts can be there.

Joseph is happy to know about eternal families.

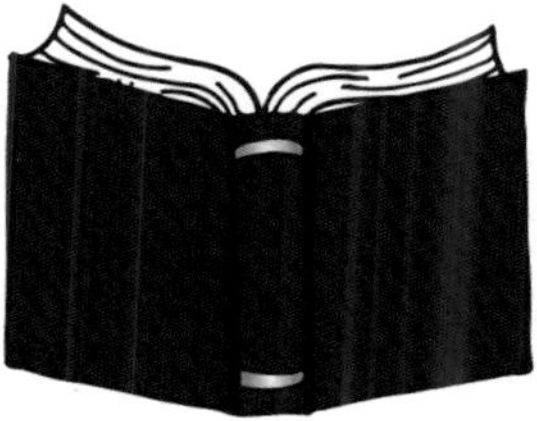

The end.

ISBN 13: 978-1-4621-4470-9

Published by CFI, an imprint of Cedar Fort, Inc. • 2373 W. 700 S., Suite 100, Springville, UT 84663
Distributed by Cedar Fort, Inc., www.cedarfort.com

Library of Congress Control Number: 2024938719

Cover design and interior layout design by Shawnda T. Craig

Printed in China • Printed on acid-free paper
10 9 8 7 6 5 4 3 2 1

HELP your child read while also learning about Church history. Build your child's confidence in reading with the entire LAMB BOOKS series as they progress through each book!

MORE BOOK SETS AVAILABLE IN THE LAMB BOOKS SERIES

BOOK OF MORMON STORIES
NEW TESTAMENT STORIES
OLD TESTAMENT STORIES

FIRST GRADE READING LEVEL
APPEALS TO PRE-K – FIRST GRADE

See cedarfort.com for more uplifting children's books.

ALSO AVAILABLE AS AN EBOOK

CFI
AN IMPRINT OF CEDAR FORT, INC.

CEDAR FORT
Publishing & Media

WWW.CEDARFORT.COM
WWW.AUTHORTIFFANYTHOMAS.COM

LAMB BOOKS
Sight Reading

Joseph Dies

OOK
3

CHURCH HISTORY STORIES

LAMB
BOOKS
Sight Reading

Joseph Dies

written by Tiffany Thomas
illustrated by Nikki Casassa

CFI • An imprint of Cedar Fort, Inc. • Springville, Utah

HARD WORDS:
Carthage, Hyrum, window

PARENT TIP: Explain that "some" does not use the silent e rule. Another exception is "come."

Some Saints in Nauvoo
make bad choices.

They have to leave, and
they get mad at Joseph.

The bad Saints bring
mobs to Nauvoo.

Joseph knows he will die,
so he starts to leave.

His friends ask him to come back, so he does.

Joseph is put in Carthage Jail.
A mob attacks with guns.

Joseph, his brother Hyrum,
John Taylor, and Willard Richards
try to keep the door closed.

Hyrum is shot and killed.
John Taylor is shot and hurt.

Joseph runs to the window,
but he is shot too.

He says, "Oh Lord, my God," and falls out the window. He is dead.

Joseph was the best man
to live other than Jesus Christ.

The end.

ISBN 13: 978-1-4621-4470-9

Published by CFI, an imprint of Cedar Fort, Inc. • 2373 W. 700 S., Suite 100, Springville, UT 84663
Distributed by Cedar Fort, Inc., www.cedarfort.com

Library of Congress Control Number: 2024938719

Cover design and interior layout design by Shawnda T. Craig

Printed in China • Printed on acid-free paper
10 9 8 7 6 5 4 3 2 1

HELP your child read while also learning about Church history. Build your child's confidence in reading with the entire LAMB BOOKS series as they progress through each book!

MORE BOOK SETS AVAILABLE IN THE LAMB BOOKS SERIES

BOOK OF MORMON STORIES
NEW TESTAMENT STORIES
OLD TESTAMENT STORIES

FIRST GRADE READING LEVEL
APPEALS TO PRE-K – FIRST GRADE

See cedarfort.com for more uplifting children's books.

ALSO AVAILABLE AS AN EBOOK

CFI
AN IMPRINT OF CEDAR FORT, INC.

CEDAR FORT Publishing & Media

WWW.CEDARFORT.COM
WWW.AUTHORTIFFANYTHOMAS.COM

LAMB BOOKS Sight Reading

The Saints Go to Utah

OOK
4

CHURCH HISTORY STORIES

LAMB
BOOKS
Sight Reading

The Saints Go to Utah

written by Tiffany Thomas
illustrated by Nikki Casassa

CFI • An imprint of Cedar Fort, Inc. • Springville, Utah

HARD WORDS:

apostle, conference, pioneers

PARENT TIP: "sh" can be difficult for younger children to pronounce. Allow them to develop at their own pace for a little bit.

When Joseph dies,
the Saints are very sad.

The Apostles all come back from their missions.

Brigham Young is the leader of the Apostles.

Sidney Rigdon used to be an Apostle, but he made bad choices.

Sidney wants to be the next prophet.

There is a big conference.
Sidney speaks for a long time.

When Brigham speaks, he looks and sounds just like Joseph!

It is a sign from God that Brigham is the new prophet.

The mobs make the Saints
leave Nauvoo in the winter.

They start walking west
and gc all the way to Utah.

God helps the pioneers along the way.

The end.

ISBN 13: 978-1-4621-4470-9

Published by CFI, an imprint of Cedar Fort, Inc. • 2373 W. 700 S., Suite 100, Springville, UT 84663
Distributed by Cedar Fort, Inc., www.cedarfort.com

Library of Congress Control Number: 2024938719

Cover design and interior layout design by Shawnda T. Craig

Printed in China • Printed on acid-free paper
10 9 8 7 6 5 4 3 2 1

HELP your child read while also learning about Church history. Build your child's confidence in reading with the entire LAMB BOOKS series as they progress through each book!

MORE BOOK SETS AVAILABLE IN THE LAMB BOOKS SERIES

BOOK OF MORMON STORIES
NEW TESTAMENT STORIES
OLD TESTAMENT STORIES

FIRST GRADE READING LEVEL
APPEALS TO PRE-K – FIRST GRADE

See cedarfort.com for more uplifting children's books.

ALSO AVAILABLE AS AN EBOOK

CFI
AN IMPRINT OF CEDAR FORT, INC.

CEDAR FORT
Publishing & Media

WWW.CEDARFORT.COM
WWW.AUTHORTIFFANYTHOMAS.COM

LAMB BOOKS
Sight Reading

The Mormon Battalion

OK

HURCH HISTORY STORIES

LAMB
BOOKS
Sight Reading

The Mormon Battalion

writen by Tiffany Thomas
illustrated by Nikki Casassa

CFI • An imprint of Cedar Fort, Inc. • Springville, Utah

HARD WORDS:
United, California, battalion

PARENT TIP: Words that begin with "wh" can be tricky. Instead of sounding them out, have them become sight words to memorize.

On the way to Utah,
an army comes.

The United States is
at war with Mexico.

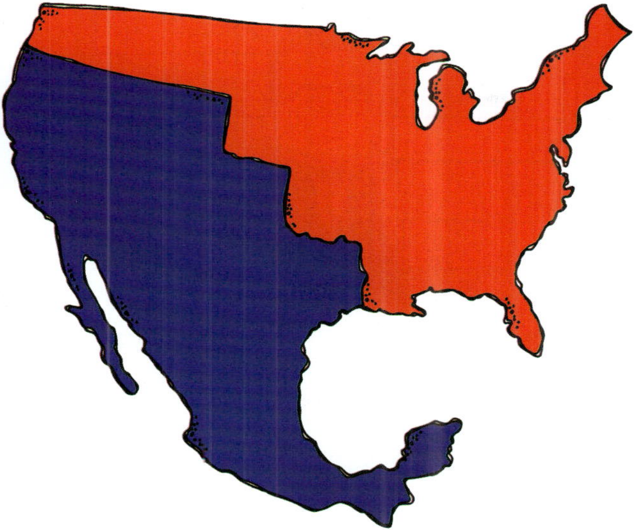

The President wants
500 Saints to fight.

Brigham tells the men to go so they can earn money.

541 men join the army.
They are the Mormon Battalion.

Brigham tells them to be good men and obey God.

It is hard for them to leave their wives and kids.

Brigham says God
will bless them all.

It is hard to be in the army.
They walk 2,000 miles to California.

They don't have to fight,
just like Brigham promised.

The men can now go find their families. They are so happy.

The end.

ISBN 13: 978-1-4621-4470-9

Published by CFI, an imprint of Cedar Fort, Inc. • 2373 W. 700 S., Suite 100, Springville, UT 84663
Distributed by Cedar Fort, Inc., www.cedarfort.com

Library of Congress Control Number: 2024938719

Cover design and interior layout design by Shawnda T. Craig

Printed in China • Printed on acid-free paper
10 9 8 7 6 5 4 3 2 1

HELP your child read while also learning about Church history. Build your child's confidence in reading with the entire LAMB BOOKS series as they progress through each book!

MORE BOOK SETS AVAILABLE IN THE LAMB BOOKS SERIES

BOOK OF MORMON STORIES
NEW TESTAMENT STORIES
OLD TESTAMENT STORIES

FIRST GRADE READING LEVEL
APPEALS TO PRE-K – FIRST GRADE

See cedarfort.com for more uplifting children's books.

ALSO AVAILABLE AS AN EBOOK

CFI
AN IMPRINT OF CEDAR FORT, INC.

CEDAR FORT Publishing & Media

WWW.CEDARFORT.COM
WWW.AUTHORTIFFANYTHOMAS.COM

LAMB BOOKS Sight Reading